I Love Myse
Do you Love Yourself?

Author: Sashalee Tomoya Edwards
Illustrator: Kiran Akram

Acknowledgement

To Paulette Doman, Peter Wilson, Margaret Mills, Louise Clarke, Magilee Daley, Wendy Miller-Mckoy other friends and family that motivated and cheered me on along the way. Everyone needs wonderful people in their lives.

Dedication

To the Lord of my life that never cease to amaze me
and inspired me to write this children story book as
I conducted Guidance class with my students at Pratville
Primary and Infant School on September 23, 2021...

To my sweet, sweet Lori Mitchellee Brown (my daughter)
keep on loving yourself as you light the world with your
own unique colours....

Let's Go To May Woods...

It was a hot summer's day and all the animals in May Woods were lazing and grazing around. They were eagerly chatting about why they loved themselves.

Lye, the loud lion was first to talk. He stood up and stretched his strong, sleek body and said, "I love myself because I have the biggest roary-roar-roar." Then he roared so loudly that the trees began to shake. All the other animals had to hold their ears at his loud, kingly roar.

Crocky, the creepy crocodile spoke next. "I love myself because I have the longest mouthy-mouth-mouth and sharpest teeth. I can catch my prey and eat it swiftly and easily." She swished and swooshed showing off her longy, long mouth.

Funky, the spunky monkey laughed and said, "This is why I love myself. I can swing from limb to limb and use my taily-tail-tail to dangle upside down." He boastfully did it for all the animals to see.

4

Jumping around on three legs, Rabby, the rabid rabbit smiled and said, "I can hippity-hop-hop higher and faster than all of you with my strong, long legs and that is why I love myself."

Pigly, the pretty piglet squealed, "I love myself because I get to eat all the food scraps around. I keep the place nice and clean with my snappy choppy mouth as I snorty-snort-snort all day long."

Finally, it was Timmy, the timid turtle's time to tell why he loved himself. Before he could say a word everyone started laughing.

Crocky the creepy crocodile asked, "Timmy, the timid turtle, is there anything to love about yourself? We know that all you do each day is splishy-splash-splash in the dark, murky, purky pond and is always late with your slow-mo-flow."

8

Timmy, the timid turtle gave a smirky smile and said, "I know something that you don't know about me and this is why I love myself."

"Well, well," croaked Crocky, the creepy crocodile, "We all know everything about you. You are so unbelievable at times." Timmy, the timid turtle blurted out, "I know that I can beat Rabby, the rabid rabbit in the second race!"

10

"The second race!" exclaimed everyone in surprise.

"Yes," answered Timmy, the timid turtle, "the second race."

"Ok, I really want to see this," said Lye, the loud lion."
Nevertheless, we already know who the winner is going to be."

Funky, the spunky monkey, swung from limb to limb laughing and said, "Timmy, the timid turtle, please don't waste our time. You know you can't beat Rabby, the rabid rabbit with your slow-mo-flow."

"Yes, I can and yes I will," said Timmy, the timid turtle confidently, while inching away with a smirky smile.

Timmy, the timid turtle's confidence got Rabby, the rabid rabbit so angry. He stomped his foot so hard, dust flew in the air. "No, you can't, and no, you definitely will not!" he shouted.

"Race, race, race!" All the animals gathered around and chanted "Race, race, race!"

"Ok, let's waste some time," Rabby, the rabid rabbit muttered haughtily." I bet I can beat you in a very short race from the pawpaw tree to the tamarind tree. And just so you don't feel too bad about your slow-mo-flow; I will slow my pace so much that you can keep up before I beat you at the first race."

"Ok," Timmy, the timid turtle replied, knowing that at a footrace he did not stand a chance against Rabby, the rabid rabbit. But little did Rabby, the rabid rabbit know that Timmy, the timid turtle could beat him at a different kind of race that he mischievously called the second race.

14

Rabby, the rabid rabbit and Timmy, the timid turtle took their places. Pigly, the pretty piglet took her tickly, prickly stick and drew the starting line while Crocky, the creepy crocodile drew the finish line.

Crocky, the creepy crocodile instructed the racers, "At the count of three, you must go." So Crocky, the creepy crocodile lifted her head a notch and croaked, "One". Then she lifted her head a second notch and croaked, "Two". Finally, she lifted her head a third notch and croaked, "Three, go!"

And they were off! Rabby, the rabid rabbit took off like a bolt of lightning while Timmy, the timid turtle crawled off in his slow-mo-flow style.

Everyone had to look twice to see that he was actually moving. All the animals cheered on Rabby, the rabid rabbit right to the finish line and celebrated his big win.

Rabby, the rabid rabbit hopped back to where Timmy, the timid turtle had merely walked a few feet away from the starting line. He burst out in laughter and said, "You couldn't even run a race to save your own life!" Rabby, the rabid rabbit looked very confused as he realized that Timmy, the timid turtle was still smiling even though he had lost the race.

Timmy, the timid turtle said, "You are boasting because you beat me in the first race but, I bet you can't beat me in the second race." Rabby, the rabid rabbit, with much pomp and pride argued," I can, and I will beat you in any and every race slow-mo; I'll win in the second, third or hundredth race."

All the other animals quickly gathered around and asked each other, "What's the second race?"

19

Timmy, the timid turtle smiled as he saw their puzzled faces. He was glad that everyone believed that Rabby, the rabid rabbit was right.

All the animals were excited to see what the second race was but had to wait until the next day as their frolic was interrupted by a sudden down pour of rain. Everyone, except Timmy, the timid turtle made a swift dash for home.

The next morning, right after breakfast, all the animals gathered around excitedly to watch Rabby, the rabid rabbit beat Timmy, the timid turtle a second time.

They were walking around and asking each other, "What's the second race?"

Lye, the loud lion asked Pigly, the pretty piglet, "Do you think that there is such a thing called the second race or is Timmy, the timid turtle up to his old tricks again?"

"I am not sure!" exclaimed Pigly, the pretty piglet, "But let's wait and see!"

Timmy, the timid turtle explained, "The second race is a race to our homes. We will race to our houses and the first one to get into his house will be known as 'Champion Racer of May Woods."

Rabby, the rabid rabbit laughed mockingly and said, "I already have that title Mr. Cracky-back. This time I will hippity, hop, hop at my full speed so that next week you will still be creepy crawling in your slow-mo-flow yet, still not reaching your house."

Rabby, the rabid rabbit's pronouncement caused a loud outburst of laughter. Pigly, the pretty piglet did a somersault and a split. Funky, the spunky monkey danced upside down by his tail and Crocky, the creepy crocodile swished-swooshed her fat tail spraying everyone with water. Even Timmy, the timid turtle, was laughing.

Once again, Pigly, the pretty piglet, drew the starting line with her prickly, tickly stick, from where they were standing at the tamarind tree. Crocky, the creepy crocodile drew the finish line in front of the dark, murky, purky pond where Timmy the timid turtle was always seen hanging out right next to Rabby, the rabid rabbit's hole in the old, cold tree stump.

Once again, Crocky, the creepy crocodile croaked, "One," and lifted her head up a notch. "Two," and lifted her head up a second notch. "Three," and lifted her head up a third notch. "Go!"

Off bolted Rabby, the rabid rabbit. Hippity, hop, hopping as fast as he could. Meanwhile, Timmy, the timid turtle quickly pulled his little turtle feet into his shell. Then he pulled his little turtle head into his shell, until only his little turtle shell could be seen. He did this long before Rabby, the rabid rabbit reached the finish line and into his house.

At the sound of his voice, Timmy, the timid turtle pushed his head and feet out of his shell and answered, "No, my friend, I won. You lost, because I reached into my house long before you reached yours."

28

"Timmy, the timid turtle, speak the truth now!" roared Lye, the loud lion. "Once again you lost and Rabby, the rabid rabbit won. We saw it with our very own eyes."

As they argued among themselves, Oak, the odd, old owl, who was always sleeping was rudely awakened by Funky, the spunky monkey. "This better be good, Funky, the spunky monkey, for there is a high price to pay for waking me up at this brilliantly, bright, blinding hour of the day."

As Oak, the odd, old owl landed on the branch of a dark lush leafy mango tree, everyone was hushed. No one dared to speak since Oak, the odd, old owl was highly respected as the wisest creature among them all. Whenever there were important matters to be discussed, they would go to him for his wise advice.

Oak, the odd, old owl listened as Lye, the loud lion explained what had happened. He leaned his head to one side, then he leaned it to the other side. He pulled down his spectacles then he pulled them back up. "Hmmm, let's see," he hooted. "Aaah, my children, it's clear. Rabby, the rabid rabbit, won the first race but Timmy, the timid turtle won the second race."

Funky, the spunky monkey amazed scratched his head. Looking utterly confused he complained, "But we saw with our very own eyes when Rabby, the rabid rabbit crossed the finish line and stepped into his house, while Timmy, the timid turtle did not run to his dark, murky, purky pond house."

"Because he did not want to lose the second race, he hid in his hard shelly-shell-shell long before Rabby, the rabid rabbit reached the finish line and into his house," squealed Pigly, the pretty piglet.

"Ah hah!" exclaimed Oak, the odd, old owl, laughing as he rubbed his tummy-tum-tum. Timmy, the timid turtle kept smiling all the while but said nothing.

Oak, the odd, old owl went on explaining, "That dark, murky, purky pond is not Timmy, the timid turtle's house. It's just where he goes to cool out when he is hotty-hot-hot. Timmy, the timid turtle never leaves his house because he carries it on his back wherever he goes. That's what makes him move in his slow-mo-flow. Because he put his head and feet in his house before Rabby, the rabid rabbit finished the race, he won.

Oak, the odd, old owl opening his wisdom book with his stick in hand said, "You see my friends, even though we are alike in many ways, every creature is different and have their own unique features.

For example, did you know that, Lye, the loud lion is very strong, have powerful muscles, teeth and jaws?

Crocky, the creepy crocodile also has powerful jaws and is able to keep his ears, nose and eyes above the water while the rest of his body is discretely covered under the water.

Funky, the spunky monkey likes to stay clean, eat plants as well as animals and has hands that can grasp anything.

Pigly, the pretty piglet's eyesight is very poor but she is sharp in her ability to smell. Among the animals that are domesticated she's the smartest of them all. She's even known to be smarter than a dog."

As he scratched his head he continued, "Rabby, the rabid rabbit has very sharp teeth that is always growing as long as he lives. He also has very strong and big hind legs.

Timmy, the timid turtle can outlive all of us as he can live very, very long even up to one hundred years. He can be very weighty even weighing over a thousand pounds.

And owls like me can turn our heads almost all around, we can see very, very far and our hearing is extremely sharp.

Therefore, we should love ourselves just the way we are and learn to appreciate the unique differences in other creatures. Never, ever compare yourself to anyone and always strive to become the best that you can be.

This is why we should love ourselves because we are all unique in our very own special way. Every single day you should think of something positive about yourself and do not allow others negative behaviour to affect you.

You must first and always believe in yourself. Never, ever look down on others and never look down on yourself. Instead, always think the best of others and always think the best about you.

After Oak, the odd, old owl had finished explaining why we should love ourselves, all the animals including Rabby, the rabid rabbit started to laugh. They finally understood the second race and how Timmy, the timid turtle won that day. They were also very glad to finally know why he walked in his slow-mo-flow.

"I have an idea," cried Lye, the loud lion.
"Let's play a ring-game while singing our
sing-along-song.

'I love me and that's how it should be
You love you and that's truer than true
I love you, because you are just you
You love me because I am just me'

Lye, the loud lion continued, "We can take
turns going in the ring to show our unique
shimmy-shim-shuwee!"

Pigly, the pretty piglet clapped, squealed with
glee and asked, "Timmy, the timid turtle can
we have more fun tomorrow learning about
why we should love ourselves?" A laughing
Timmy, the timid turtle replied "Oh yes, Pigly,
the pretty piglet, we definitely can and we will
continue tomorrow."

42

The animals were having so much fun playing when, amidst the hot summer sun, suddenly a burst of rain showered down. Everyone helter-skeltered to find their homes.

Timmy, the timid turtle then shouted, "Hey guys, wait a minute. I love me and my slow-mo-flow. I can take my shelly shell house wherever I goey-go-go!" Then Timmy, the timid turtle pulled in his little turtle feet and his little turtle head as he curled up cozily in his little shelly-shell bed.
Sleepily he sang,

'I love me and that's how it should be
You love you and that's truer than true
I love you, because you are just you
You love me because I am just me'

Soon Timmy, the timid turtle fell fast asleepy-sleep-sleep while the rainy-raindrops played tip-a-tappa-tap on his shelly house top.

Fun Facts About Our May Woods Friends

Turtles can be found right across the world. They are some of the oldest animals around. Their shells are not exoskeleton and there are approximately 200 species of turtles. They have a second shell and are not silent as you may think. They shed their first baby tooth around an hour after they are hatched.

Lions live in a family called groups or pride depending on the amount of their food and water supply they will stay together. Hunting is conducted largely by the lionesses (female lion). When the female lions are out hunting for food the male lions protect the cubs and their territory.

Owls necks can rotate up to 270 degrees. Parliament is a term used to describe a group of owl. Some owls hunt other owls. They are very good hunters. There are some owls that does not hoot.

Pigs though normally seen dirty are really clean animals by nature; they roll in the mud because it makes their bodies feel very cool. Male pigs are called boar while the females are called sow. Pigs are not hunters; they eat what they are fed or what they find while roaming.

Rabbits are sociable creatures that live in groups. The male rabbit is known as a buck while the female is known as a doe. Their eyes are positioned to the sides of their heads. They have fun leaping in the air.

Crocodiles are long livers and are feared by most creatures. They are actually earth's largest reptiles. They produce tears and can see very good at nights.

Monkeys can live up to 50 years; there are over 200 types in our world. They have tails unlike their cousins the ape. Did you Know these fun facts?

Did you Know these fun facts?

Expanding My Vocabulary

Amazed – To be surprised or filled with astonishment

Boastful - Demonstrating a large amount of pride and satisfaction in your

accomplishments, property, or skills.

Confident – Having a positive feeling as it relates to one's ability to successfully achieve goals or aspirations.

Cozy – A comfortable safe and relaxing feeling.

Creepy – An uncomfortable, fearful or unpleasant feeling.

Curious – The desire to strongly know about somewhere, someone or something.

Dangle - To freely move in a hanging motion.

Graze – A term used for animals eating grass that is growing in an open area.

Habitat – An area where certain plant is found or animal live

Lush – A pleasant thick overgrowth of trees, vegetation or flowers.

Mysterious – Hard to communicate or comprehend; different, unusual in a strange way.

Outburst – An unexpected excessive display of an emotion in a negative way.

Prey – The food that is hunted and eaten by animals.

Rabid – Very angry or violent.

Somersault - A complete overturn of one's body with the head down and the feet in an upward position.

Timid – To be shy or fearful, not bold.

I am sure you can find a lot more spell words in the story.

Rhyme Time

Tickly	Prickly	Lazed	Grazed
Funky	Spunky	Timmy	Timid
Murky	Purky	Rabby	Rabid

Will you help me find some more rhyming words in the story?

Descriptive Words or Phrase

Timid - Timmy   Rabid – Rabbit   Loud – Lye

Odd Old Owl   Creepy – Crocodile   Bright-Hour

Funky – Monkey   Smirky – Smile   Loud - Roar

Snappy, choppy mouth   Strong, long legs   Pretty, Pink Piglet

Can you help me find some more descriptive words in the story?

Word Tense - Present, Past, Continuous

Graze	Grazed	Grazing
Laze	Lazed	Lazing
Sleep	Slept	Sleeping
Hop	Hopped	Hopping
Crawl	Crawled	Crawling

Can you help me find some more words and place them under the correct tense?

Printed in Great Britain
by Amazon

82580172R00031